fantastic ideas for
nursery gardens

FEATHERSTONE

FEATHERSTONE

Bloomsbury Publishing Plc
50 Bedford Square, London, WC1B 3DP, UK

BLOOMSBURY, FEATHERSTONE and the Feather logo are trademarks of Bloomsbury Publishing Plc
First published in Great Britain 2018 by Bloomsbury Publishing Plc
Text copyright © June O'Sullivan and Clodagh Halse, 2018
Photographs © LEYF 2018 / © Shutterstock, 2018

A catalogue record for this book is available from the British Library

ISBN: PB: 978-1-4729-5303-2; ePDF: 978-1-4729-5304-9

2 4 6 8 10 9 7 5 3 1

Printed and bound in India by Replika Press Pvt. Ltd.

To find out more about our authors and books visit **www.bloomsbury.com** and sign up for our newsletters

Contents

Introduction

> *If children's developing sense of self becomes disconnected from the natural world, then nature comes to be seen as something to be controlled or dominated rather than loved and preserved.*
>
> R. White, 2004

Froebel coined the term 'kindergarten' when, looking down from the top of a hill, he declared that this would be a garden for children. Since then, the benefits of the nursery garden for children's emotional, social and cognitive development have been widely accepted. Of course, staff benefit from having access to a lovely garden too! Interestingly, the Welsh word for 'children' is 'plant', a connection that is beautifully serendipitous. Children and plants respond similarly. Put them in the right place, with the right people who will nurture them in the right way, and they will thrive.

Children love being outside and their visible delight is a joy to behold. Staff sometimes struggle to get the balance right between the outside classroom and a 'garden of delight'. There is no need to worry; a well-stocked, well-kept garden will offer the children a huge range of learning opportunities. Sensitive, knowledgeable staff can provide multiple learning experiences for children whether planting seeds, making a daisy chain or using grass, mud and leaves to create a dinosaur swamp!

The natural environment inspires learning through deeper engagement. In a survey of schools that had improved their grounds, 65% reported an improved attitude to learning, 73% an improvement in behaviour and 64% a reduction in bullying. 84% of schools noticed improvements in social interaction while 85% reported an increase in healthy active play (*Learning Through Landscapes, National School Grounds Survey, 2003*).

Most nurseries depend on any naturally green-fingered staff they have or those willing to learn some basic gardening skills. Regular gardening may seem like a chore to busy staff but the benefits outweigh the challenges, given our responsibilities to:

* enrich children's skills and knowledge by broadening their horizons

* increase their interest

* open up wider opportunities

* extend language and contribute to deeper conversations.

Gardening, no matter how simple, can help children progress in all these areas. Gardening helps observant children as they watch the daily and seasonal changes. Gardens are places where we learn to care about plants and protect wildlife. It opens up a caring side which benefits personal, social and emotional wellbeing.

Gardening isn't hard: the secret is choosing the right plants and putting them in the right spot, with the right soil and conditions. Remember to watch the plants, water them, especially those in pots and, when more confident, try growing plants from seed. Children use all their senses when gardening. Celebrate their sense of delight as you watch and teach them to become the gardeners of the future as they sow, tend and harvest their plants.

> *The love of gardening is a seed once sown that never dies.*
>
> Gertrude Jekell

The structure of the book

This book is all about gardening with children. It is more than a list of learning opportunities for the outdoors; it is a set of activities to introduce the joys of gardening.

What you need: Plants that grow healthily. Many of the activities list suitable plants. There is also a list of other child-friendly plants on this website: **https://www.rhs.org.uk/education-learning/gardening-children-schools**

Essential tools to keep your nursery garden clean and safe

- Garden gloves
- A rake and a trowel
- A spade and fork
- Shears
- Pair of secateurs
- Lawn mower (if you have grass)
- Outdoor sweeping brush

What to do: follow the step-by-step instructions carefully. Most importantly, look after the plants after they have been planted. Water them and protect them from weather extremes and pests.

Top tips are helpful hints to make an activity work well and have been learned from experience!

Taking it forward helps you consider how to extend the learning and includes additional gardening activities.

What's in it for the children? reminds you (and others), briefly, how the suggested activities contribute to learning in the Early Years Foundation Stage.

Health & Safety

Never allow children access to water unsupervised as they can drown in less than 2 cm of water. Avoid ponds, but if you already have one, place a safety grid across it. Having said this, water play and watering plants are fun activities for children and just the sort of activity that is perfect outside. So teach children the rules of the garden: this will go a long way to mitigating accidents and create the right balance of risk and fun.

Poisonous Plants
Most plants are perfectly safe to touch or even to put in the mouth. The effects from eating poisonous plants are stomach ache, vomiting and diarrhoea and can be easily treated. Seek medical advice if you are concerned. Generally, the seeds and berries are the most poisonous parts of the plants and flowers and leaves are the least toxic part. Touching some leaves or, more specifically, the sap can cause allergic reactions. Beware of some plants that sting (nettles) and others that have thorns (pyracantha) or grasses (cortaderia) with sharp, serrated leaf edges. For a list of harmful plants see: **https://www.rhs.org.uk/Advice/Profile?PID=524**

Make a butterfly garden

Watch them flutter by

What you need:

- Good 'host plants' providing food and shelter for caterpillars including bird's-foot trefoil and potentilla
- Shrubs to provide nectar and attract butterflies such as buddleia (this produces lilac flowers from late Spring well into Autumn but can get very large!)
- Different coloured flowers especially purple, pink and yellow such as zinnia, verbena, wallflowers and aubretia
- Herbs such as lavender, parsley, rosemary and chives
- Caterpillars – wild or bought in from **www.insectlore.co.uk**
- A jar
- Fresh nettle
- Cabbage leaves
- Twigs
- An old pair of tights and an elastic band
- Sugar and warm water

What to do:

1. Plant 'host plants' for the caterpillars and butterflies.
2. Research and find out about the most common butterflies in your area. Many butterflies are under threat so talk to the children about this and how to look after them. The top three most common butterflies in London include: Meadow Brown, Large Skipper and Adonis Blue.
3. Make a planting plan. Remember to choose a light, sunny space and water the plants regularly.
4. Find some caterpillars on cabbage plants or nettles nearby. Ask children and parents to look in their gardens. Alternatively, buy some online. Keep the caterpillars in a jar out of direct sunlight with fresh nettles and cabbage leaves for food and a twig to climb. Cover the jar with an old pair of tights secured with an elastic band.
5. Let the children help clean out the jar and add fresh food every two to three days.
6. When a caterpillar is ready to change, it will climb up high, curl up and then turn into a chrysalis. Put the jar in a quiet place and try not to disturb it. It normally takes about two weeks before the chrysalis hatches into a butterfly.
7. When it first emerges, the butterfly may look a little 'squashed'. Over the next hour it will stretch and dry its wings ready for its first flight.
8. You can feed the butterflies sugared water before letting them go. Dissolve 1 teaspoon of sugar in 10 teaspoons of warm water and put this in a lid near to the butterflies.
9. Take the children to the butterfly garden to release the butterflies and invite parents to join you.

Top tip ⭐

Help the children to look out for butterflies laying eggs on host plants so that the cycle can continue.

What's in it for the children?

Learning about the life cycle of a butterfly and how to care for butterflies. Using lots of new vocabulary and observation skills.

Taking it forward

- Place some flat stones in the garden for butterflies to use for basking in the sun, spreading their wings and raising their body temperature so they are able to fly and remain active.

- This is also a great observation zone for the children to come and make sketches, paintings and take photographs of the butterflies. Have magnifying glasses, binoculars, paper and pens available so they can draw what they see.

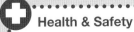 **Health & Safety**

Most smooth caterpillars are safe to handle – the hairy ones can cause irritation.

Fast food for bees

Create a garden habitat or 'bee takeaway'

What you need:

- Bee-friendly plants with nectar (bee carbohydrate) and pollen (bee protein) such as honeysuckle, aquilegia, jasmine, hyssop, thistle, Sweet William, verbena
- Terracotta pot
- Dry straw
- Chicken wire
- Plastic piping
- Needle
- Slate or heavy stone

Top tip ⭐

Encourage children and families to get involved in the annual Great British Bee Count, organised by Friends of the Earth.

What's in it for the children?

Learning all about the life cycle of a bee and discovering how important bees are to agriculture and ecology will help children see how vital it is to care for them.

Taking it forward

- Introduce the children to how bees make honey and organise a special honey-themed 'Bee Tea Party' with family and friends.

✚ Health & Safety

If a child has a known allergy keep them away from the bee garden. If a child is stung take immediate first aid precautions.

What to do:

1. It is important for children to learn about the benefits of bees as many bee species are now declining or extinct. Invite an expert to talk to them about the importance of protecting bees.

2. There are six main types of bumblebees in the UK. Start by introducing the children to those so they can learn the difference and tell them apart from wasps.

3. Consider whether you want to help bees nest. Generally, bees like a dry, concealed cavity – often underground. They can use disused rodent's nests.

4. Make a bee nest. Use an old terracotta plant pot, filled with dry straw and some chicken wire to keep it in place, though not packed too tightly. Perforate an old piece of piping with drainage holes using a needle. Push the pipe into the centre of the pot so one end sits in the nest, allowing the bees to climb in and out of their home easily.

5. Bury the pot about one third into the ground to create the cool, moist conditions bees need. Choose a safe space away from the children's main play area.

6. Make sure the pipe is straight so it has a clear entrance and exit tunnel. Put a slate or heavy stone on the pot to keep it dry.

7. Alternatively, buy a nest from the gardening shop or a bee conservation website.

8. Create an observation space where the children can sit, watch and look out for the arrival of the bees. Help them to understand how bees operate so they keep safe but are not frightened.

The daily dig

What you need:

- Accessible space with plenty of soil, sand or mud
- Small child-size tools: spades, forks, rakes, sieves, etc.
- Treasures to hide
- A rota

Top tip ⭐

Digging may seem like a rather ordinary activity but it's a wonderful way for children to use all their physical skills.

What's in it for the children?

Handling tools and digging soil will develop gross motor control, coordination and body strength, alongside effort, bravery and imagination!

Taking it forward

- This is a great place to develop children's creativity. Challenge the children to dig in rows, dig holes, create hills and valleys, etc.
- Hide some shiny stones, crystals, shells and other interesting objects and let their imaginations run riot.

✚ Health & Safety

Make sure children wash their hands after playing in the digging area.

What to do:

1. When designing and shaping the nursery garden, include a digging area. This is exclusively for digging, but be prepared for children to add sand, stones, twigs and whatever interests them.

2. Don't try to grow anything in the area. Let the children enjoy the digging experience.

3. Explain to the children that the digging area will be a place for them to regularly practise handling tools, digging and turning the soil, and finding things.

4. Prepare an area of ground with easy access.

5. Show children the tools they can use in the digging area.

6. Draw up a rota so that all the children can take turns.

Grow your own herb garden

Sow, grow, pick and eat

What you need:

- A dry sunny space to grow herbs like sage, basil, oregano, coriander, thyme, chives, rosemary and lavender
- A shady spot for other herbs: mint, parsley, rocket, chervil and sweet cicely
- A five litre pot (plants dry out too quickly in small pots)
- Other containers including old bins, wheelbarrows, boxes, sinks, tyres, etc.
- Crocks (broken terracotta), grit or gravel for drainage
- Sand, compost

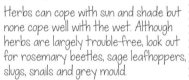

Top tip ★

Herbs can cope with sun and shade but none cope well with the wet. Although herbs are largely trouble-free, look out for rosemary beetles, sage leafhoppers, slugs, snails and grey mould.

What's in it for the children?

Growing herbs involves a wide range of the different sensory experiences, alongside physical skills used for planting, watering, pruning and picking the herbs.

Taking it forward

- Harvest lavender seeds at season end. Place a spoonful in a square of muslin, scrunch up the corners and tie with a length of ribbon.

- Thyme is an evergreen herb and can be picked all year. Its distinctive taste goes well with many dishes. You could tie a sprig with ribbon and hang it up for decoration.

What to do:

1. Choose the right space to set-up your herb garden; whether in the ground, a container or in a window box. Read the instructions carefully as some herbs love the sun while others can cope in semi-shade.

2. Herbs grow well in containers. Mint really spreads so is best confined to a pot. Make sure you have drainage holes in the pots. Add some crocks (broken terracotta) or grit to the bottom.

3. Herbs don't need very rich soil so mix some sand in the compost (about half and half) before planting.

4. Water well but not too much! Some herbs don't like too much water as they are used to growing in dry conditions.

5. You can grow herbs from seeds but it may be a challenge for the busy nursery teacher! Sage is a good herb to try growing from seed.

6. Buy young healthy looking plants and don't overcrowd them.

7. Choose herbs that the children can eat so they can pick them to add to food such as basil for pizza, oregano for soups and salads, mint for potato salad and tea, and parsley for most things!

8. Introduce the herbs to the children and get them to rub them between their thumb and forefinger so they can smell their scent.

9. Create a watering and picking rota as herbs need to be picked so they don't go to seed.

Start a stumpery
A home for plants and minibeasts

What you need:

- Photos of a stumpery
- Paper and pencils
- Whole tree stumps (from dead or pruned trees)
- Logs and branches (not too large or long)
- Pieces of bark
- Worked timber such as railway sleepers or floorboards
- Moss
- Compost
- Suitable plants include ferns, vinca, brunnera and hostas

Top tip ⭐

The stumpery shouldn't require much attention once built so it's a good long term feature in your garden.

What's in it for the children?

Seeing their design develop into a place full of plants and minibeasts will give children a sense of achievement.

Taking it forward

- Photograph each stage of the stumpery construction. Treat it as an ongoing live project so the children can go on 'stumpery watch' to observe changes as the plants take hold and the minibeasts start to move into the crevices.

What to do:

1. Look at photos of a 'stumpery' (a garden feature similar to a rockery) online. Explain to the children that it is made of tree stumps and other wood. Involve children in planning and designing the stumpery on paper first.

2. Collect old logs from the park, abandoned in gardens or purchase from a garden centre.

3. Ask parents to help bring branches or logs from their gardens. Show them the design so they can see what you need.

4. Identify where you intend to place your stumpery. Dark and shady parts of the garden work best.

5. Encourage the children to think about the shape of their design so minibeasts can live among the plants.

6. Design the stumpery so you can use the holes and crevices in the stumps or logs. Line the holes with moss to retain moisture. Add compost and then plant ferns directly into some holes.

7. Try planting vinca so it trails over the logs and place a brunnera in the shade between the logs. If you include hostas, plant them high up, with grit around the plant to deter the slugs that they will inevitably attract.

The coming of Spring

Watching the garden transform

What you need:

- Early flowering Spring bulbs and bedding plants: dwarf daffodils, grape hyacinths, snowdrops, pansies, primulas, hellebores
- Old wooden fruit or vegetable crates
- Terracotta pots, colanders, old teapots, baskets, sinks, etc.
- Hessian (really good liner)
- Crocks (broken terracotta), gravel or grit for drainage
- Peat free compost
- Small gardening gloves
- Child-size tools: trowels, forks, watering cans
- Camera, paper and pencils

What to do:

1. Celebrate the coming of Spring by planting a Spring garden in a container. After the Winter, children will enjoy watching the flowers emerge.

2. Plan a trip to a local garden centre and choose some suitable small Spring plants. Enjoy saying and learning the names of different flowers.

3. Back at your setting, select a suitable container. Almost anything will work and the children will enjoy choosing their own depending on the type of garden they have in mind.

4. Line the container with hessian and add drainage if necessary.

5. Fill with peat free compost.

6. Talk about position, colour, balance and space around the plants before you plant them.

7. Dig holes in the compost and add the plants carefully, firming down afterwards.

8. Water them regularly and position the container in a sunny spot away from cold winds.

9. Create a display of the process (either photos or drawings) and encourage children to talk to their families about planting a Spring container at home.

Top tip ⭐

Check out your local garden centre. Some will donate plants and containers free to nurseries and schools.

What's in it for the children?

The children will enjoy choosing the container and planning which flowers to plant. A trip to the local garden centre will be a great opportunity to learn the names of plants and how to care for them.

Taking it forward

- Decorate the containers by painting with Spring colours.

- Try sketching or painting the Spring Flower arrangements to take home and cheer up the kitchen.

50 fantastic ideas for a nursery garden

Build a raised bed
Constructing outside

What you need:

- Willing volunteers!
- Bricks, wooden pallets, logs, planks or fencing
- Bedding plants and annuals
- Soil to fill the base
- Topsoil for the top section to supply plants with nutrients
- Farmyard manure
- Flowers, vegetables

Top tip

This activity could be popular with local businesses who want to get involved in the community so use your networking skills!

What's in it for the children?

Children particularly enjoy activities which involve visitors coming to the nursery. They will learn a lot from observing and being involved in the construction process.

Taking it forward

- Invite the local press to visit your setting and write an article. Send photos of the project to some nursery trade magazines.
- Children can role play being the builders, wearing hard hats, drawing plans, using clipboards, taking photos and so on.

What to do:

1. Building a raised bed is a good way to combat some tricky problems that nursery settings may face: limited space, rather dark gardens, awkward shapes or poor soil. They can be built waist high, which is a good height for young children, and it also enables staff with bad backs to be involved. (Back injuries are one of the highest causes of absence in the Early Years sector!)

2. Explain your plans to the children, parents and carers and ask for volunteers to help with the construction. Contact local voluntary agencies or charities who may like to be involved, such as The Prince's Trust. A friendly local builder might also be helpful.

3. Ensure the dimensions of the beds are appropriate to the children using them.

4. Build the beds using bricks if possible as they last longer.

5. Alternatively use wooden pallets, logs and planks.

6. Another option is to construct a second skin or layer of bricks 25 cm apart. Try planting bedding plants and annuals in the space this creates.

7. Fill the bed up with soil and add a layer of topsoil and manure on the top.

8. Plant the raised bed with flowers or vegetables. See 'A vegetable plot' on p.36 for some good ideas on what to plant.

Garden in a bottle

Recycle, sow and grow

What you need:

- Images of bottle gardens
- Empty plastic water bottles
- A sharp knife (adult use)
- Sandpaper
- Multi-purpose compost
- Plant plugs: (small-sized seedlings) Busy Lizzies, small ferns, geraniums and vinca
- Bottle cap
- Two nails

Top tip

Hang them in the entrance to the nursery where they can cheer up the space, capture families' and visitors' interest and become a talking point.

What's in it for the children?

This activity combines recycling and gardening. Children will be closely involved with caring for the plants and helping them to grow.

Taking it forward

- Plant a bottle garden in a sunny place and fill it with the nectar-loving flowers so popular with butterflies, see 'Make a butterfly garden', p.6.

- These bottle gardens would make great gifts or items to sell at fundraising events or fairs.

✚ Health & Safety

Make sure children are supervised when handling sharp tools.

What to do:

1. Look at some images of bottle gardens online. Talk about how using plastic bottles is a good way to combine recycling and growing plants. It is easy to collect lots of suitable bottles.

2. To make the bottle garden, turn the bottle on its side and pierce a small hole or two for drainage.

3. Cut an oval shape out of the other side of the bottle. Use sandpaper to remove any sharp edges.

4. Fill about two thirds full with multi-purpose compost.

5. Add your plant plugs. Choose suitable plants that cope well in either shade or sun, depending on where the bottles are going to end up.

6. Pierce the bottle cap so the water can drain.

7. Water and trim the plants regularly.

8. Attach several to a wall or a shelving unit by hanging on nails.

Hang it in the window
Make a window box or hanging basket

What you need:

- Images of window boxes and hanging baskets
- Collection of containers that fit safely on the window ledge or balcony
- Crocks (broken terracotta) for drainage
- Hanging basket with a liner
- Potting compost
- Plants and flowers suitable for window boxes or hanging baskets such as miniature conifers, annuals, lamb's ears, herbs, lettuce, kale, verbena, coral bells, coleus and trailing plants such as lobelia and fuchsia
- Hook

What to do:

1. Show the children some images of window boxes and hanging baskets online. Go on a walk around the neighbourhood and look out for some good examples.
2. Explain that these miniature gardens are a good way to bring the garden into the nursery especially if there is a shortage of outdoor space. If window ledges are low, even the youngest children can see the flowers, smell them and watch them grow.
3. Design and decorate the window box and/or basket.
4. Line the bottom of the box with crocks to ensure drainage.
5. Put a liner in the basket.
6. Use potting compost to fill them both.
7. Loosen and wet the roots of the plants before planting.
8. Arrange the plants following the design, allowing some space between plants to spread.
9. Water weekly.
10. Place the window boxes in an accessible place for children and visitors to enjoy. Hang the basket in the entrance for everybody to appreciate.

Top tip ⭐

Window boxes can have a range of objects, not just flowers! Let the children come up with some ideas.

What's in it for the children?

Encourage conversation and observation as children choose plants, selecting a range of one colour or types of plants, vegetables or herbs.

Taking it forward

- This would be a great opportunity for a competition between the rooms or among nurseries if you are part of a nursery group or affiliated to local schools. Challenge groups to plant the most creative, interesting or quirky version.

50 fantastic ideas for a nursery garden

A prickly garden
Handle with care

What you need:

- Cacti and succulents
- Child-size gardening gloves
- Crocks (broken terracotta)
- Large plant pot, not too deep
- Shingle and coarse sand or grit
- Compost
- A few pebbles
- Watering can with a sprinkler

Top tip

The prickly garden captures the children's imagination but may make adults worry about children getting scratched. However, it's worth remembering that children learn more deeply when they are involved in the whole learning activity.

What's in it for the children?

Introducing children to desert plant life and nature's ways of storing water is an early science experience.

Taking it forward

- Help children to research how these plants survive in their natural habitat and find out about other wild life that lives in deserts or areas of severe drought.

✚ Health & Safety

Take care with the thorns and prickles; some are extremely sharp! Others are dangerous because they enter the skin like a splinter, but cannot be seen, which makes removal difficult.

What to do:

1. Show the children some cactus plants and talk to them about creating a prickly garden. Remind them to handle the plants with care, preferably with gloves on, so they don't get scratched!

2. Organise a trip to the local garden centre to choose plants from the cactus family for the prickly garden. Although these plants are generally grown for their beautiful foliage, some will flower too.

3. Ask the children to place some crocks in the base of the pot. Cover them with a layer of shingle or coarse sand. This is to provide the plants with good drainage.

4. Mix some coarse sand into the compost and fill the pot almost to the top.

5. Sort the plants into those with prickles and thorns and those without. Carefully take the non-prickly plants out of their pots and plant them into the large prepared pot. Make sure there is enough soil around the roots – plants like to feel safe and firm in their new home, not loose and floppy!

6. Now for the prickly ones. The children need to pick them up wearing gloves or by wrapping a folded sheet of newspaper around each one, so that they don't get the prickles in their fingers. Ask them to plant them in the pot and carefully firm them in.

7. Place pebbles in the spaces between the plants and use the sand and shingle to cover any remaining soil.

8. Water the pot gently using a watering can with a sprinkler end on it.

9. Place the prickly garden on a windowsill and wait, patiently, for it to start growing! The garden will only need to be watered when the soil is dry. These plants come from places where water is extremely rare!

The mud kitchen

Messy fun outdoors

What you need:

- Old kitchen sinks, cupboards, bowls
- Mud
- Kitchen utensils
- Saucepans
- Potato mashers
- Sieves
- Whisks
- Garlic press
- Pestle and mortar
- Wooden juicer
- Honey dipper
- Turkey baster
- Pastry brush
- Twigs, stones, leaves, cones, petals, etc.
- Vegetables, herbs, spices

What to do:

1. A mud kitchen is now a regular feature in many nurseries. Its look will vary depending on the available equipment and space.

2. Managing the mud can be tricky so cordon off the space and let the mud dry out before cleaning up.

3. Set up the kitchen just like a real kitchen. Be creative with the items you provide.

4. Collect natural materials such as twigs, stones, leaves, vegetables, petals, etc. The options are endless.

5. Let children use small amounts of vegetables, herbs and spices in their mud creations.

6. Provide adequate work space so that the children can stir, mix, cook and create potions, lotions and concoctions!

Top tip ⭐

Sometimes the most popular spot in the nursery gets overused so keep it regularly topped up with mud and plenty of cooking utensils.

The freedom to make a mess and create different mixtures will be enjoyed by the children as they practise control and coordination and develop their motor skills.

Taking it forward

- Encourage children to think of fantastical names for their potions and tasty names for their culinary creations.

✚ Health & Safety

Provide plastic gloves for any children with sensitive skin conditions. Make sure all the children wash their hands after playing in the mud kitchen.

 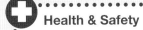

Herby boots

These boots are made for planting

What you need:

- Old welly boots
- Drill (adult use)
- Grit
- Compost and sand
- Selection of herbs
- Shelf or suitable place to display them
- Lolly sticks or tongue depressors

Top tip ⭐

Look around your setting for other containers that could be recycled into mini-gardens such as cracked teapots, old buckets or old watering cans.

What's in it for the children?

Creative use of unwanted boots and the power of recycling is a powerful message. This activity also provides hands on experience with herbs, their different uses, tastes and scents.

Taking it forward

- Herbs are beautiful to look at but even nicer to add to meals. Take photos of the children picking the herbs and adding them to their food, such as sprinkling parsley onto tomatoes, adding mint to water, sprinkling lavender on cupcakes.

What to do:

1. Ask children to bring in old welly boots and make a collection of different-sized boots. There will probably be some old boots in your setting that can be recycled too. Even better if they already have holes in the soles!

2. Drill holes in the soles of the boots and add some grit for drainage.

3. Fill with potting compost mixed with a bit of sand.

4. Choose some suitable herbs. Mint, parsley and chervil cope with some shade. Basil, oregano, sage, thyme and rosemary need sun. For more information see 'Grow your own herb garden' on p.10.

5. Plant the herbs in the top of the boots.

6. Write the names of the herbs on lolly sticks, tongue depressors or larger pieces of balsa wood and stick next to the plants.

Grass jungle
Where adventure is created

What you need:

- *We're going on a Bear Hunt* by Michael Rosen

- A sunny spot with light, moist but well-drained, moderately fertile soil

- A selection of ornamental grasses

- Golden sedge is one variety that will do well either in full sun or partial shade

- Cortaderia has blue tones

- Stipa and deschampsia are easy to grow and quite prolific. (Keep them under control by weeding out and pruning)

Top tip ⭐

Don't worry if the grass gets trampled underfoot and loses its height. It is very hardy and copes well and should spring back to life especially after rainfall.

What's in it for the children?

This activity combines the love of stories with gardening and will inspire lots of conversations about sound, colour and texture.

Taking it forward

- Grow some 'grass people' where the grass becomes the hair. Fill a paper cup or pot with soil, sprinkle grass seed on top. Draw a face on the cup. Water until the green grass hair starts to grow!

What to do:

1. Read *We're going on a Bear Hunt* by Michael Rosen. Enjoy the word sounds of 'swishing' and 'swashing' through the grass.

2. Choose a spot where you can grow three different grasses together so they create a jungle for the children to go on a 'bear hunt'.

3. Choose the grasses most suited to the environment. Most ornamental grasses tolerate a wide range of conditions. Ask at the local garden centre or do some research.

4. Plant them according to the instructions on the packaging as some prefer sun to shade.

5. Grasses need to be watered frequently especially in the dry weather.

A magical garden

Where imagination leads the way

What you need:

- Twigs, bark, leaves
- Pebbles and stones
- Shells, glitter, bells, shiny material
- Small world figures
- Small plastic animals
- Small plants or annuals
- Tyre, wheelbarrow, wooden crate, shallow plant pot, tin bath
- Soil
- Drill (adult use) or crocks

What to do:

1. Talk to the children about different types of gardens that feature in stories, films, etc.

2. Engage the children in designing a magical garden. What do they think it should include?

3. Go on a nature walk to gather the items in the local park, woodland or gardens. Collect twigs, bark, leaves, pebbles, stones and anything else that might be used.

4. Provide other 'magical' items for children to use including shells, glitter, bells, windmills and shiny materials.

5. Choose a few small pot plants or annuals such as violas, pansies or cyclamen.

6. Build the garden inside a tyre, wheelbarrow, wooden box, shallow plant pot or old tin bath.

7. Fill the area with soil. Make sure you drill holes or add crocks if necessary to allow the soil to drain.

8. Alternatively, create an enclosed safe space such as round the bottom of a tree or under a bush.

Top tip ★

Don't worry about the children getting dirty while they play. Let their imaginations lead the way. They can infuse a stone or a leaf with fantastical powers that they can use to amaze adults!

What's in it for the children?

The magical garden will provide opportunities for children to take part in free and unstructured imaginative play alongside nature.

Taking it forward

- Write a book about the fairies, elves and other magical creatures that might visit your garden and all their adventures. Make some peg doll fairies using old-fashioned pegs, pipe cleaners, net wings, etc.

Building dens

What you need:

- Old branches, pallets, crates, offcuts of wood, large planters, etc.
- Notepads and pens
- String, tape, pegs
- Fabric, towels, sheets
- Cushions, pillows, duvets, beanbags for comfort
- Small tables, boxes for storage
- Fairy lights

What to do:

1. Every nursery needs a den to play in. Outside dens can be built from branches, sticks, wooden pallets, crates, offcuts of wood, etc. Go on a walk to the local park to collect found items for the den.

2. Help the children design the den and draw a plan. When building the den, remind the children to regularly check the plans against the emerging edifice. Encourage them to consider whether they need to alter their plans.

3. What else can they find to add to their den? Use pieces of fabric, towels or sheets to make curtains, doors and dividers.

4. Use cupboards, tables and boxes for added storage.

5. To make it comfortable inside, provide cushions, pillows, duvets and beanbags. Can the children think of any other ways to make the den cosier or even darker?

6. Add magic items such as fairy lights and special objects – whatever the children want to have in their den!

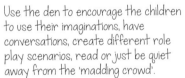

Top tip ⭐

Use the den to encourage the children to use their imaginations, have conversations, create different role play scenarios, read or just be quiet away from the 'madding crowd'.

What's in it for the children?

Children will use lots of physical skills to manoeuvre the bigger resources and build with different materials. They will work cooperatively and use new vocabulary as they build their shared den.

Taking it forward

- Photograph the building process and make a simple book featuring the stages to completion. Read *Sally's Secret* by Shirley Hughes – a good story about building a den.

A sensory garden
All five senses

What you need:

- **Sight:** sunflowers, marigolds, snapdragons, Sweet William, hydrangeas, heuchera

- **Taste:** radishes, lettuces, tomatoes, beans, cucumbers and rocket; herbs such as nasturtium petals, mint, rosemary, chives, basil

- **Sound:** love-in-a-mist, bamboo, buddleia, hebe, salvia, alliums, penstamon and snap dragons; grasses such as briza maxima (great quaking grass), oriental miscanthus

- **Touch:** stachys lamb's ear (stachys byzantina), thistles, African sundew, saxifrages, silver sage, houseleek

- **Smell:** curry plant, lemon scented verbena, pelargonium, lavender, chocolate cosmos, sweet peas, geraniums, rosemary, mint

What to do:

1. Encourage the children to help design the garden by introducing them to plants which stimulate all five senses.

2. **Sight:** Plant lots of brightly-coloured flowers and shrubs.

3. **Taste:** Mix and match fruit, vegetables and herbs. Try some quick growing vegetables such as radishes and lettuces for a fast harvest. Add nasturtium flowers and leaves to salads and serve mint in water or with potatoes.

4. **Sound:** Many plants attract buzzing bees and fluttering butterflies. Grasses make a rustling sound. Love-in-the-mist forms puffy seed-heads that rattle when shaken. Bamboo stems can be knocked together to make music.

5. **Touch:** Rub the furry leaves of the lamb's ear, the sharp leaves of the thistle or the sundew that uses sticky leaves to catch its prey.

6. **Smell:** Many plants have a strong scent but flowers only smell when blooming, so choose plants with scented leaves such as the curry plant or lemon balm. Allow the children to brush past the plant or pick a leaf and rub it between their fingers to release the scent.

7. This Is a long term project. Once the garden is growing it becomes a teaching space.

8. Teach children the names and features of the plants and make a book of the sensory garden to show to families and visitors.

What's in it for the children?

The science of plants and how they benefit us will be an important part of the learning experience.

Taking it forward

- Teach the children more detail about the plants they are choosing to grow. Think about tasty plants, encouraging seed dispersal, smells to attract insects, sharp spines to deter pests, furry leaves to protect plants from extreme weather and succulents that store water.

- Make some wind chimes by cutting and hanging different lengths of bamboo on trees around the garden so they knock together in the wind.

Top tip ⭐

Consider the impact of the sensory garden on some of the children. If you have a child with limited eyesight or poor hearing, plant more of the flowers and shrubs that will enhance their experiences.

The compost bin

Recycling food and plant waste to feed your garden

What you need:

- A compost bin with a lid or a wooden compost bin made from pallets
- Old plant waste
- Kitchen waste
- Soil
- Old piece of carpet or doormat
- Small child-size tools: spades, forks, rakes

What to do:

1. In a world with finite resources we need to teach children about looking after the environment. Composting is an easy way to help children understand how to manage food waste as they see it compost down into nutrient-rich soil.

2. Involve the children and their families at every level of planning and constructing the compost bin.

3. Contact the local council waste and refuse department to ask about obtaining a compost bin for your setting. Alternatively, build your own compost bin using four wooden pallets turned on their sides to form a square. Make sure the bin is placed on earth and not concrete.

4. Fill the bin with dead leaves, green waste from the garden, old plants or weeds, waste from the hamster's cage (if you have one!), fruit and vegetable peelings from the kitchen – even eggshells. Don't put in cooked food as it may attract rodents. Sprinkle some soil on the top.

5. Cover the bin with an old piece of carpet or a doormat to keep the heat in and leave it alone until you have some more waste to add.

6. After three or four months remove the cover and get the children to dig the compost over. Leave it to rot down further.

7. When the bottom of the compost is brown and crumbly, it's ready. Dig it into the garden – the plants will be really pleased!

Top tip ★

Create a visual display board to show children and remind parents what can go in a compost bin.

What's in it for the children?

Food waste is a real issue and by helping children understand about it at an early age they will be more interested in recycling and environmental issues.

Taking it forward

- Encourage families to have a go at making a compost bin at home at the same time.

A plastic bottle greenhouse

A project for the whole family

What you need:

- Willing friends and family!
- Approximately 1,400 empty 2 litre plastic bottles without labels (to build a greenhouse that is 8' x 6')
- Wood to build a frame
- Bamboo garden canes or sticks
- Pegs and hammer (adult use)
- Bubble wrap (lots)

Top tip ⭐

There are several videos online showing how to build bottle greenhouses which will help with this project.

What's in it for the children?

This activity gets children involved in designing and building a structure using lots of physical skills, alongside learning about recycling and the mighty power of cooperating and working together.

Taking it forward

- Use the greenhouse to propagate seedlings and start growing suitable plants such as cucumbers and chillies. Share the story with local gardening and community clubs. Celebrate with a grand greenhouse opening and invite the local press.

What to do:

1. This activity is designed to be part of a family or volunteer project. Working in partnership with home and nursery is the basis of quality practice.

2. Finding activities that involve different people at different stages is a great idea. This activity involves some people saving bottles, others planning the greenhouse and a few actually building it.

3. Wash all the bottles in the water tray to remove labels. Children will enjoy helping with this.

4. Cut off the bottoms and remove the bottle lids.

5. Decide on the frame for the greenhouse, wood is probably best.

6. Thread your bottles through a bamboo cane or lengths of stick to hold them in place. Use 10 or 12 bottles per cane.

7. Peg your canes onto the frame and hammer them in place.

8. Insulate your roof with bubble wrap to reduce draughts.

9. Install your greenhouse in a place where it is protected from high winds.

10. This is a most cost effective way of building a greenhouse. There are gaps at the tops of the bottles so it becomes self-watering as heavy rain can enter where the bottles are lying side-by-side.

The great minibeast hunt

Explore, discover, learn

What you need:

- Books, pictures and plastic models of minibeasts
- Magnifying glasses or magnifying pots
- Torches
- Suitable habitats

What's in it for the children?

Searching for minibeasts requires good observation and fine motor skills. Children will also gain lots of new vocabulary and an understanding of the science of habitats.

Taking it forward

- Keep a group minibeast diary for a week and then create a display to show families and visitors what the children have learned. Involve families by suggesting weekend activities to spot and record selected minibeasts.

What to do:

1. The great minibeast hunt is a favourite activity in the nursery garden and children are usually keen to join in, although they may not want to get too close to the worms. However, try to be brave and model good practice by not squealing or panicking at the sight of a wasp or a spider.

2. Invite the children to be scientific explorers seeking to understand what lives in their garden.

3. In preparation, look at pictures in books and online of the minibeasts they want to find.

4. Talk about likely habitats and places to look such as underneath stones and plants, in holes in the ground, on or under leaves, under the bark of trees, and so on.

5. Take a magnifying glass or torch and look in the dark places in the garden or wherever you might find insects.

6. Introduce as many names of insects and associated words as you can. Explain that the children can be 'lepidopterists' – studying or collecting butterflies and moths or 'entomologists' – studying insects.

A bug hotel

A temporary home for bugs on the go

What you need:

- Paper and pens
- Wooden pallet or frame
- Dead wood, bark, pine cones, wood chips
- Bamboo, reeds, drilled logs
- Stones, tiles, old terracotta pots
- Dry leaves, sticks, twigs, straw, moss
- Old roof tiles or planks, roofing felt
- Nectar-rich flowers

Top tip

You can buy a bug hotel but it's more fun to make one!

What's in it for the children?

With hedges and old walls falling down, the cracks and crevices that bugs use to shelter, live and breed in are being destroyed so the bug hotel is a simple way for children to get involved with conservation and recycling.

Taking it forward

- Choose a suitable name for your hotel and put a sign up outside.
- Ask children to observe the comings and goings at the hotel and record what they see.

What to do:

1. You can often find a bug hotel in the nursery garden, usually situated in a dark place or in the wildlife corner.
2. Collect together all the resources you will need to make a multi-storey bug hotel.
3. Get the children to draw up plans for the design of the hotel. You can make it as simple or complicated as time and resources allow.
4. Use a wooden pallet or wooden frame for the main structure. It needs to be sturdy with gaps and placed on bricks to allow the air to circulate.
5. Fill in the gaps with dead wood and loose bark for beetles, centipedes, spiders and woodlice.
6. Create small holes using small tubes (not plastic) made out of bamboo, reeds and drilled logs for solitary bees.
7. Leave some larger holes with stones and tiles to provide the cool, damp conditions frogs and toads prefer.
8. Use dry leaves, sticks or straw for ladybirds and other beetles.
9. Add a roof to keep it relatively dry. Use old roof tiles or some old planks covered with roofing felt.
10. Surround your hotel with nectar-rich flowers – essential food for butterflies, bees and other pollinating insects.

Feed the birds
Show them you care

What you need:

- Weighing scales
- 100 g of shredded suet (from any supermarket)
- Saucepan
- Cooker
- 100 g of wild birdseed mix (from a pet shop)
- Extra tasty additions – fresh peanuts (hulled from monkey nuts, not toasted, roasted or salted), sunflower seeds, stale cake crumbs, cheese crumbs
- Seeds extracted from dock, thistle, stinging nettle, knapweed, teasel or ragwort collected from the wilder parts of your garden
- Wooden spoon
- A small tin (washed and dried) or a coconut shell
- String
- Binoculars
- Observation diary

What to do:

1. Ask children to weigh out an amount of suet and put it in a saucepan. Help them to melt it over a gentle heat.
2. Weigh out an equal quantity of birdseed mix.
3. Add in any extra ingredients they wish to include.
4. When the fat is liquid, turn off the heat. Remove the pan from the cooker and stir in the seeds and other ingredients.
5. Mix together carefully with a wooden spoon.
6. The mixture should be quite sticky so it binds together once it's cool. Leave it to cool slightly.
7. Tip or spoon it into the tin or the coconut shell. Leave to set completely.
8. Once set, add string to the tin or shell and wedge it into the branch of a tree in the garden.
9. Place it somewhere the children can see it easily. Let children use binoculars to watch the birds close up. Keep an observation diary and take photos of the birds feeding.
10. Children can learn the names and descriptions of birds that will be attracted to your garden if it provides food, water and shelter. Provide them with plenty of books to identify the birds.

Top tip ⭐

Encourage the children and their families to take part in the Big Garden Birdwatch run annually by the RSPB.

➕ Health & Safety

Be aware of children in the nursery who may have nut allergies. You may decide not to use nuts in this project.

What's in it for the children?

Learning about wildlife and looking after birds will develop children's understanding of the world. The science of cooking involves maths and measurement and is also very satisfying.

Taking it forward

- Let children fill individual cupcake cases or plastic cups with the mixture and take home to put in their garden at home.

- Birds will be attracted to your garden if it provides food, water and shelter, especially in the Autumn and Winter when food is scarce. Make a display for children and parents with useful questions and information: Did you know young birds can easily choke on dry peanuts and stale bread? Did you know birds love a shallow bowl of water that they can drink and bathe in?

The wormery

A home for wiggly worms

What you need:

- A large, clean, glass jar with a lid
- Sand
- Moist soil
- Earthworms
- Old leaves
- Vegetable peelings, tea leaves, overripe fruit
- Some black paper and a cool, dark cupboard

Top tip

Try not to be squeamish about worms. Charles Darwin studied them for 39 years and concluded that life on earth would not be possible without them!

What's in it for the children?

They will learn about the benefits that worms bring to the soil, the eco system and why gardeners love them.

Taking it forward

- Children can learn about the two main types of worm: earthworms (found in the garden) and tiger worms (found in compost).

- Observe the worms closely and encourage children to describe them. Can they tell which end is which? How? Can they describe how a worm moves? Can they see the hairs on the worm's skin?

What to do:

1. Many adults are not great fans of worms but accept that they are an important part of the eco system.

2. A wormery or a worm bin is an easy and efficient system of converting ordinary kitchen waste into liquid feed and rich organic compost through the natural action of worms.

3. Put a layer of sand at the bottom of the jar, about 1 cm deep.

4. Add a thick layer of soil, then add another thin layer of sand, then another thick layer of soil. Ensure there is about 5 cm of space left at the top.

5. Organise a worm hunt around the garden or in the park. Where do the children think they will find the worms? Remind them that worms like the dark so that's where you will find them. Look under stones, in holes in the flower beds and in the grass after a shower of rain.

6. Put the worms into the jar then add some old leaves, vegetable peelings, tea leaves and overripe fruit.

7. Pierce a couple of holes in the lid and screw it on the jar.

8. Place a cover of black paper around the jar and put it into a cool, dark cupboard. Worms 'breathe' through their skin which must be damp and not too cold.

9. Leave it for a couple of weeks and then observe what the worms are doing. What has changed? Are there worm patterns in the earth? Have they eaten the vegetables and fruit peelings?

10. Always ensure the contents of the jar are moist, not too wet and definitely not too dry.

Tracking snails

Finding, identifying and trailing snails

What you need:

- Access to a garden or outdoor area with lots of snails
- White correction fluid or brightly-coloured nail varnish

Top tip ⭐

Finding a way to turn a gardening task into a fun activity is useful especially when children learn about the positives and negatives of garden wildlife.

What's in it for the children?

Tracking wildlife in the garden brings science to life and will inspire them to want to find out more.

Taking it forward

- Ask children to find out more about snails and produce fact sheets.
- Introduce the children to the work of Henri Matisse (*The Snail*) and help them become snail artists!

 Health & Safety

Ensure children wash their hands carefully after handling the snails.

What to do:

1. There are many reasons that gardeners track snails, not least to stop them using their 100 tiny teeth to eat the plants.

2. Help the children to find some snails in the nursery garden. Look on and around plants, walls and in the undergrowth.

3. Each time the children find a snail, ask them to put a dot of white correction fluid or nail varnish carefully on the top of its shell. Hold on to it while the correction fluid dries.

4. Make different marks on each snail so they can be identified later. Children could use their initials.

5. Take the marked snails out of the garden, but not too far away – as snails move very slowly.

6. Over the next few days, encourage the children to keep an eye out in the garden to see if they find any snails with correction fluid/nail varnish on their shells.

7. If any snails do find their way back to their original territory, the children will know that snails have a homing instinct. If not, they have just found out an amazing thing – how to get rid of snails!

Dinosaur swamp

Learning all about dinosaurs

What you need:

- Aprons or old clothes
- A muddy or shady spot
- A builder's tuff spot or water tray
- Mud or sand
- Water
- Natural materials: stones, twigs, leaves, ferns, small branches, grass, mud (anything from the garden that will hide the dinosaurs and make the swamp swampier!)
- Lots of toy dinosaurs
- Fishing nets or sieves

What's in it for the children?

These simple sensory experiences are a source of rich language and conversation opportunities and will inspire some very imaginative play.

Taking it forward

- The swamp can be adapted to house other toy creatures – mammals, insects or fish.

- Categorise the dinosaurs so the children understand the difference between herbivores and carnivores. Learn about the time periods, e.g. Jurassic and Cretaceous. Get the children to identify the flying dinosaurs and those who lived in water. Help children make their own dinosaur factsheets.

What to do:

1. Find a good muddy space in the garden or put the tuff spot or water tray in a shady spot.

2. Line the tray with mud or damp sand.

3. Add some water to create a swampy texture.

4. Fill the tray with stones, sticks and leaves from ferns. Explain to children that ferns were around when the dinosaurs roamed the earth.

5. Place the dinosaurs in the tray. Introduce lots of dinosaur vocabulary including the correct names of dinosaurs such as 'Velociraptor' or 'Stegosaurus'.

6. Provide children with fishing nets or sieves so they can fish for swamp creatures.

7. Encourage the children to be as creative as they like in their imaginary play.

Top tip

Read some dinosaur stories to the children to fire up their imaginative play. Try 'Harry and the Bucketful of Dinosaurs' by Ian Whybrow, 'There's a Dinosaur in My Bathtub' by Catalina Echeverri and 'Tom and the Island of Dinosaurs' by Ian Beck.

Potatoes in a bag

Growing and eating food from the garden

What you need:

- Multi-purpose or peat free compost
- 8 litre polythene sacks
- Potato tubers (try small potatoes that are more resistant to pests such as Maris Bard, Athlete or Casablanca)
- Plant food or high potassium fertiliser

Top tip ⭐

More experienced gardeners may like to count tubers into egg boxes with the children and leave for a few weeks until green shoots appear – 'chitting' before planting, as this ensures a better harvest.

What's in it for the children?

Potatoes are relatively easy to grow and children can be involved in the whole process – planting them, watching them grow, digging them up, washing them and eating them.

Taking it forward

- Create a potato menu and list all the different ways to cook and serve potatoes. Share this with families.
- Create a potato display with all the different types of potato from sweet potatoes and baking potatoes to little new potatoes.

What to do:

1. Potatoes can be grown in soil but as many nursery gardens are small it's often easier to grow them in a bag, which is much easier for novice gardeners.
2. Put 15 cm of compost in the polythene sack and put a single potato tuber in the middle. Then cover with compost until it's about 5 or 6 cm from the rim.
3. Keep the compost moist.
4. Feed weekly with high potassium fertiliser.
5. During the winter, put the bag in a greenhouse or a sunny hall and then when the frost is over place it outside. Keep an eye out for late frosts, as the potatoes may need 'earthing up' which is adding more compost on top to protect them.
6. Watch out for when the bag becomes bulgy, as this is a sign that the potatoes have grown.

A vegetable plot

Planting, growing and caring for vegetables

What you need:

- Plants
- Grow bags
- Bamboo canes and twine for bean frames
- Containers
- Child-size gardening gloves
- Child-size tools: hoes, forks, spades and trowels

What to do:

1. Vegetables can be grown in well turned soil, raised beds, containers or grow bags. The choice of where you grow will depend on the available space and amount of sun and shade.

2. Choose your plants carefully. A plant will always do well if it is placed in the right spot and is looked after.

3. It's fine to grow vegetables in grow bags. Tomatoes, aubergines, sweet peppers and cucumbers do especially well in a sunny spot. Keep them well watered and fed.

4. For peas and beans, construct an A-Frame or teepee-shaped frame from bamboo canes. Use gardening twine or wire to hold the frame in place.

5. If you are growing in containers then large pots are best. Mini vegetables such as peppers, spring onions, radishes and lettuce, thrive in containers. Salad leaves grow well in small containers or window boxes.

6. Involve families in this gardening challenge. Ask them to help in the nursery or to plant similar vegetables at home.

Top tip ⭐

Tools need to be stored safely indoors and cleaned after use.

What's in it for the children?

Working together to grow a variety of vegetables will increase their understanding of caring for plants and the environment.

Taking it forward

- Create a diary 'from earth to table' for the different vegetables.

- Who can grow the most tomatoes, the longest bean or the fattest cucumber?

- Make some vegetable soup or do a simple stir-fry with the children. Provide some recipes for parents to cook at home with the vegetables you have grown at nursery. This will reinforce what the children have learned and encourage healthy eating.

Super sunflowers

Plant, grow and measure

What you need:

- Different varieties of sunflower seed: Teddy Bear (60–90 cm), Valentine (1.5 m) or Soraya (2 m)
- Child-size gardening gloves
- Child-size trowels, rakes
- Plastic bottles
- Bamboo or wooden stakes to support the tall sunflowers
- Plant labels and pencils
- Ruler, measuring tape

Top tip ⭐

Create a sunflower height chart and track the growth weekly. Involve families. Present a prize for the tallest!

What's in it for the children?

Taking ownership of individual plants will increase the children's involvement and awareness of the growing process. Caring for the plants and comparing measurements will help them to observe change.

Taking it forward

- Introduce children to books that feature sunflowers such as *Katie and the Sunflowers* by James Mayhew.
- Make honey roasted sunflower seeds and serve them for snack.
- Let children plant individual sunflower seeds in pots to take home.

What to do:

1. The sunflower (helianthus annuus) challenge should be part of every child's nursery experience, whether you choose sunflowers that grow very tall or miniature.

2. Sunflower seeds can be sown straight into the ground where they are going to grow, so make sure the space you are going to sow is weed free. Show the children how to use a trowel to remove the weeds.

3. Rake the soil to a fine tilth (fine crumbly texture) and make some drills 12 mm deep. Leave a 10 cm space between each seed.

4. Plant the seeds carefully and cover them with soil. Don't forget to water them!

5. If the plants become crowded, thin them out to about 45 cm apart leaving the strongest, tallest plants.

6. Be careful, as slugs and snails like to eat the new shoots. Protect the seedlings by cutting the tops off plastic bottles and placing them on top.

7. As the sunflowers begin to grow taller, support them by loosely tying a cane against the stem.

8. Let the children label their sunflowers and measure them.

Blackberry jam for tea

Making yummy home-made jam

What you need:

- 350 g of blackberries
- Empty jam jars with lids (sterilised)
- 25 ml of water
- Juice of a lemon
- Saucepan
- Cooker
- 350 g of preserving sugar
- Wooden spoon
- Knob of butter

Top tip

Take care picking the berries. The bushes are prickly and surrounded by nettles and the juice stains clothes.

What's in it for the children?

Talking with the children about how the fruit is picked and then transformed into a jam introduces some scientific concepts and new language.

Taking it forward

- There are many fruits from which to make jam. Check out which bushes or plants are growing nearby such as gooseberries, redcurrants, cherries or rhubarb. Jam can be made with many different fruits so give it a try.

✚ Health & Safety

If the blackberries are hand-picked from wild, it is worth soaking the fruit in salted water for a couple of hours to clean them and destroy any bugs. After soaking rinse well in clean water.

What to do:

1. This is a group activity where children can be involved in picking blackberries and either making the jam at home or bringing the berries to nursery to make jam together.

2. Take the children to a local park, hedgerows or country lane to find blackberry bushes. Look for fruit that is just ripe rather than too soft. Pick the fruit carefully and make sure you wash it before eating or cooking with it.

3. This recipe makes two jars of jam. Prepare the jars and ensure they are clean by sterilising them in a warm oven at 140°C for 10 minutes.

4. Place the blackberries, water and lemon juice into a large, heavy-bottomed saucepan and place on the hob on a low heat.

5. When the blackberries are soft add the sugar and fold it into the fruit until dissolved.

6. Let the children take turns to stir the mixture gently.

7. Bring the fruit to a gentle boil, stirring occasionally and let the fruit simmer for about 10–12 minutes (adults only).

8. Remove the saucepan from the heat. Place a knob of butter on top of the fruit and stir across the top to break down the froth or foam on the surface. Skim any excess off with a spoon.

9. Test for setting point by placing a small amount of jam onto a cold plate. If it wrinkles when you push it with your finger it's ready.

10. If the jam is still runny, place the pan back onto heat and boil gently for a further 2 minutes. Test again.

11. Pour the mixture into the sterilised jars and place lids on immediately. Allow to cool and store in a dark place ready to be tried the next day!

Elderflower cordial
Infusing and creating cordial

What you need:

- 30 elderflower heads
- 1.7 litres/3 pints boiling water
- 900 g castor sugar
- Large mixing bowl
- Wooden spoon
- 50 g citric acid (available from chemists)
- 3 unwaxed lemons (zest and fruit)
- Strainer
- Empty bottles

Top tip ⭐

Elderflower tastes delicious, but once it's in the kitchen waiting to be turned into cordial don't be put off by its strong slightly unpleasant scent.

What's in it for the children?

Picking, washing, stirring and observing all the changes involved in this process are invaluable early science experiences.

Taking it forward

- Invite children to design labels for the bottles. They can be sold at the summer fair to raise funds.

- This is a lovely activity to involve parents. Ask them to help provide the elderflowers. Share the recipe and organise an elderflower tea party. The children can make invitation cards decorated with elderflowers.

What to do:

1. One of the nicest drinks in early summer is a glass of cold elderflower cordial served diluted with either water, soda water or lemonade. It's also tasty poured over ice cream or used in cakes.

2. Elderflower grows wild in gardens, parks, wasteland and especially by water. The heads are in bloom from April to May. Ask parents, friends and families if they have elder trees in their gardens and could supply some blooms.

3. Pick the freshest and most flowery heads to make the cordial.

4. Carefully wash the elderflowers to remove any dirt or bugs. The children could help with this in the water tray.

5. Pour the boiling water over the sugar in a very large mixing bowl and stir until the sugar dissolves.

6. Add the citric acid, the lemon slices and zest and then the flowers.

7. Leave in a cool place to infuse for 24 hours, stirring occasionally.

8. Strain through some muslin or a colander lined with a tea towel and transfer to sterilised bottles.

50 fantastic ideas for a nursery garden

I spy in the garden

Being in the garden

What you need:

- Binoculars (either real or made from cardboard tubes)
- Magnifying glasses and pots
- Stopwatch

What to do:

1. Even the smallest of gardens is full of interesting things for children to find and record.

2. Children love playing hide and seek, playing detective and seeking treasure. As many children have become detached from the natural world it is important to find as many ways to reconnect as possible.

3. The rules of 'I spy' are familiar to most of us. It is a straightforward game that encourages observation and concentration.

4. Start with the traditional version: 'I spy with my little eye, something beginning with… (use the name and the sound of the letter)'. Add sign language for the first letter to include all the children.

5. Try 'I spy with my little eye something that flutters by'.

6. Try 'I spy with my little eye something that makes a buzzing sound'.

7. Try 'I spy with my little eye something that is wiggly and long'.

8. The list is endless. Encourage the children to come up with challenges for each other to spot.

9. Introduce new rules to the game and make it more challenging, e.g. using a stopwatch or 'find it before I count to ten!'.

Top tip ⭐

Start with easy items to spot and then increase the level of difficulty or complexity.

What's in it for the children?

'I spy' is a simple game but it encourages listening, observation, concentration, language and phonics skills and if you put the children in pairs or groups, even teamwork.

Taking it forward

- Children may want to record their findings for you to use as the basis of a display or a book or to share with their family. Include photos and sketches drawn by the children.

We're going on a scavenger hunt

Searching in the garden

What you need:

- Scavenger hunt list:

  Colours: find an example of all the colours in the rainbow

  Shapes: find an example of a circle, square, triangle, rectangle, diamond, star, spiral

  Alphabet: find something beginning with each letter of the alphabet

  Leaves: find orange leaves, pointy or prickly leaves, star-shaped leaves

- Pen or pencil
- Clipboard (optional)
- Bag or box to collect items in
- Whistle or timer
- Prize

What to do:

1. A scavenger hunt can work well even in the smallest garden. It's great for groups, families or just a few children.

2. The thrill of the hunt can be enhanced by staff instilling some excitement as the children are told about their task. Make it magical because in the end it's not just the finding of the treasure that's fun, it's the seeking.

3. Divide the children into pairs, teams or groups.

4. Show them the hunt list and read through it together. Be clear what you want them to do. Do you want them to pick a leaf and put it in a bag or simply call out or tick it against the picture of the item on the list?

5. Use a whistle or a timer to start and stop the activity.

Top tip ⭐

This is different from a treasure hunt because you don't have to spend ages making clues. Just ask the children to find items that already exist in the garden.

What's in it for the children?

Working together in pairs or as part of a group will require children to listen carefully, follow instructions and work cooperatively.

Taking it forward

- Scavenger hunts can be repeated again and again. Each time children will find different treasures. Include more imaginative tasks such as seeking a magic stone or discovering a new colour!

- Help them to manage their fears in a safe way such as fear of the dark or getting stuck or lost. Try a scavenger hunt at dusk and provide children with torches.

➕ **Health & Safety**

Make sure a member of staff is nearby at all times to help children and prevent accidents.

Tell me a story

Inspiring imagination outside

What you need:

- A storytelling tree or chair
- A comfy, cosy, quiet space
- A story
- Props from the garden stones, leaves, trees, flowers, wildlife

:Top tip ⭐

A story told without a book has many benefits. Try and weave children's names into the story as you are telling it and include some familiar points of reference. They will love hearing the name of their school and their friends' names as the story unfolds.

What's in it for the children?

Listening and concentrating on stories will help children to understand how a story works with a beginning, middle and end and develop their own storytelling skills.

Taking it forward

- Use a 'story stone' and encourage children to have a go at making up a story in the garden. They can only speak while holding the special stone.

- Practise telling stories. Try in front of a mirror at home. The more you do it the easier it gets!

What to do:

1. Invite the children to come and sit by the storytelling tree or chair in the garden, ready to listen to a story.

2. Children enjoy listening to stories from books and stories told freestyle or improvised.

3. If you lack confidence, don't be afraid to retell a traditional story such as *The Three Little Pigs*, *Jack and the Beanstalk* or *The Enormous Turnip*.

4. Start the story with a favourite opening line such as 'Once upon a time…' or 'One fine/rainy/windy day/night in the garden… at (insert name)'.

5. Use an experience that happened earlier in the day or week that children can relate to.

6. Use the garden to provide the props and the storyline. Look about and see what's happening. 'Once upon a time, we were sitting in the garden when _____ spotted a butterfly landing on the buddleia bush. She closed her wings on the purple flower and we heard her sigh and say in a quiet silvery voice…'.

Made to measure

Measuring and labelling a plan

What you need:

- Measuring tape, metre sticks, length of rope, ruler
- Paper (especially graph paper) and pencils

Top tip

Take photos of the garden first so the children can look at pictures of what they are measuring and mapping

What's in it for the children?

This activity involves lots of mathematical thinking and measurement. Drawing a plan to scale is also a challenge.

Taking it forward

- Let the children make individual plans of the garden and turn them into collages using a variety of materials, tissue paper, corrugated card, sand paper, dried flowers, moss, leaves and gravel.

- Ask the children to photograph, measure and map their gardens at home or if they don't have a garden, try a balcony, park or family garden. It's all about making and measuring, which is part of environmental learning.

What to do:

1. Explain to the children that they are going to measure the garden in order to produce a map or plan.

2. Go outside and ask the children to measure particular parts of the garden such as a flower bed, path or lawn.

3. Start with non-standard units such as children's feet: How many steps long is the lawn? How many jumps does it take to measure the path?

4. Use a range of implements to do more mathematical measuring such as a measuring tape, metre sticks or a length of rope. How will they measure some of the nooks and crannies in the garden?

5. Record the measurements and use them to make a plan of the garden space.

6. Draw a large plan to scale and make it the basis of a display in your setting. Ask children to label each part including favourite flowers, bushes, trees and garden features.

A daisy chain

Weaving jewellery made of flowers

What you need:

- A grassy lawn with lots of daisies
- A fairly long thumbnail!
- Cocktail sticks
- Lots of friends to help
- Measuring tape, ruler

What to do:

1. Choose a sunny day when the grass has not been mowed and there are lots of daisies in the garden or park.

2. Ask the children to pick a few daisies, making sure the stalks are long and thick.

3. Show them how to use their thumbnails to split the stalk about halfway down its length and make a small slit. A cocktail stick could work too.

4. Ask them to thread the stalk of another daisy through the slit, then to make a hole in the new daisy's stalk and so on.

5. Work with partners or in small groups to speed things up.

6. Keep going until there is a really long daisy chain. Measure the chains and count the daisies.

7. Turn them into rings, bracelets, crowns and necklaces.

8. Organise a competition to see who can make the longest daisy chain at home or school.

Top tip ★

Dry out the daisy chains and preserve them by hanging them in the airing cupboard or over a heater.

What's in it for the children?

This activity will require concentration and cooperation as the children work together.

Taking it forward

- Use the daisy chains to decorate the setting, drape all around tables, hang from the ceiling and on wall displays.

- Try another garden tradition. Pick a buttercup and hold it under their chin, if it shines yellow, then it's a sign that they like butter!

Conker creativity
Making art with conkers

What you need:

- Conkers
- Leaves, twigs, shells, stones and nuts
- Collecting bags
- Paper
- Hoop frame
- Camera

Top tip ⭐

Encourage the children to change their creations using the conkers and other materials again and again. The essence of this activity is that it is NOT permanent.

What's in it for the children?

They can use lots of mathematical language about size and position as they create their artwork.

Taking it forward

- Try some conker painting. Paint the conkers and use them to make prints in different colours. Try some repeating patterns.

- Line a round tray with paper. Dip the conkers into pots of paint and decorate the paper by rolling the conkers around the tray.

What to do:

1. The traditional activity with conkers is to bake them hard, thread a string through the middle and use them to beat other conkers! Try some temporary art instead inspired by the work of Andy Goldsworthy.

2. Collect some conkers and other natural materials from the garden or local park. Organise an Autumn walk with the children and their families or ask families to collect materials with the children at home and bring them to your setting.

3. Explain to the children that they can use the conkers and other materials to create a shape or design that is temporary. This can be completed inside or outside.

4. They can lay the materials out on a piece of paper, inside a hoop frame or on the grass outside.

5. Don't set any expectations for the children; let them come up with something on their own.

6. Talk to them about what they have chosen to make.

7. Take photographs of the designs and artworks to display after they have been cleared away.

Blow me a wish

Sharing wishes with dandelion seeds

What you need:

- Dandelions seed heads (freshly picked)
- A windy day
- Fans made from folded paper

What to do:

1. Sit the children in a circle. Talk about making wishes. Pass round a 'dandelion clock' and invite children to share their wishes when they hold it. Alternatively use a 'wishing star' or 'talking stick'.

2. Go outside on a windy day and encourage children to feel the impact of the wind on their bodies.

3. Make fans from folded paper so that they can feel the breeze it creates when they move the air about. Or switch on an electric fan on a hot day and feel the difference it makes.

4. Go on a dandelion hunt and find some dandelion clocks. Explain how the dandelion and other plants spread their seeds using wind dispersal so that new trees and plants grow.

5. Let the children blow the seeds off the dandelions. How far away do the seeds travel? Who can blow a seed the furthest?

6. Show them the traditional way to tell the time by counting how many blows it takes to clear the dandelion clock.

Top tip ⭐

Help the children to use blowing the seeds away as a symbol for blowing away worries.

What's in it for the children?

This activity combines the science of wind and seed dispersal with the fun of blowing away dandelion clocks.

Taking it forward

- Play 'What's the time, Mr Dandelion Clock?' in the style of 'What's the time, Mr Wolf?'

- Look at some sycamore helicopters. How do the children think these seeds move? Demonstrate the seeds spinning like mini-helicopters. Encourage the children to spin and twist their bodies and fall down on the grass.

50 fantastic ideas for a nursery garden

Leaf creatures
A leafy day of art

What you need:

- A garden, field, woodland, park
- Bags or boxes for collecting materials
- Different leaves, petals, sticks, grasses
- Paper, cardboard, wood
- Glue

What to do:

1. Explain to children that you are going to make some leaf creatures, people or animals.
2. Go on a walk together and take bags or boxes to collect leaves, petals and grasses.
3. Try setting a target such as find 10 items to create your picture.
4. Be more specific, for example, find four long green leaves and two triangular shaped leaves.
5. As you walk, talk about what you find using new and interesting words. Encourage the children to describe the leaves using different words: 'shiny', 'spiky', 'damp', 'floppy', 'speckled', 'thin', 'mottled', etc.
6. Challenge the children to describe colours in more detail. Is it bright green, bluey-green or dark green?
7. Back at your setting, use the items to create a picture of a person, animal or creature on backing paper, cardboard or wood. Stick the materials down carefully.
8. Challenge the children by suggesting that they can only use 10 or 15 objects.

Top tip ⭐

Let the children take ownership of their leaf creations by giving them a name and making up stories about them.

What's in it for the children?

Children will enjoy finding their own materials and being creative with them using their artistic skills and imagination.

Taking it forward

- Try this activity in the Autumn when the leaves are falling and there is a greater variety of colour.
- Make press prints using leaves pressed into thinly rolled out clay. Laminate leaves on strips of card to make bookmarks as gifts.
- For inspiration, look at Henri Matisse's *La Gerbe* and use paper cut-outs of leaves.

Autumn colour wheel

Creating an autumnal rainbow of leaves

What you need:

- 15 Autumn leaves of one type
- 12 narrow leaves
- One special leaf for the centre
- Collecting bags
- Camera

Top tip ⭐

Talk about leaves having different shades of colour, shapes and sizes. Try to increase children's use of poetic and descriptive language.

What's in it for the children?

This activity encourages children to see colours, shapes and sizes in detail as they examine the Autumn leaves and experiment with how to display them.

Taking it forward

- Save the work into a more permanent display. Pin or glue the leaves onto card or spray with adhesive to make them secure.

- Create an Autumn art display and present the children's work from here alongside 'Conker creativity', p.47 and 'Leaf creatures', p.50. Invite families and friends to the art show.

What to do:

1. This is a simple activity inspired by the glorious colours, shapes and tones of Autumn leaves.

2. Go on a walk in the garden or park with the children to collect suitable leaves.

3. Back at your setting, spread out the leaves on a large table and arrange in a circle.

4. Ask the children to sort the colours so they are going from light to dark and encourage them to notice the different tones and hues of the leaves.

5. Make another smaller circle inside the outer ring using a different-shaped leaf and then put a special leaf in the middle.

6. Alternatively, this arrangement can be created outside on the grass or on the floor as a temporary display to celebrate a transitory moment of Autumn glory. Don't forget to capture it in a photograph.

7. Allow groups of children to create their own versions of this artwork showing off Autumn colours, such as a rainbow of leaves or a multi-leaved tree.

The winter gardener

Planting flowers in the winter

What you need:

- Heat treated hyacinth bulbs
- Containers
- John Innes No. 2 compost
- A cold, dark place
- Black bin liners
- Water
- A bright, cool space

Top tip ⭐

Take care not to peek at the bulbs too much while they are in the dark and don't overwater.

What's in it for the children?

By observing and caring for the bulbs children will learn about how plants grow. Preparing and selling the hyacinths at a fundraising event will help children to feel part of their community.

Taking it forward

- Decorate plain pots using paints and collage materials. Use red and green colours and lots of glitter to make them look more seasonal.

✚ Health & Safety

Be aware that hyacinths cause stomach upset if ingested. Wear gloves when handling the bulbs as they can aggravate skin allergies.

What to do:

1. Just because it's cold doesn't mean that the garden is out of bounds. In fact, growing plants for a plant stall or the Christmas Fair is a good source of fundraising.

2. Try planting hyacinth bulbs in September/October. These are fragrant pot plants that will be ready to bloom for Christmas.

3. Visit the local garden centre to buy bulbs or order online.

4. Choose a variety of containers such as cups, mugs, boxes, jugs and pots. Fill them with damp compost.

5. Set the bulbs in the compost so that the top of the bulb shows at the surface.

6. Place in a cold, dark place such as a cellar, garage or shed for about ten weeks.

7. Cover them in black bin liners to stop any light getting through. Check the bulbs regularly and water sparingly if the compost feels dry.

8. Once shoots appear, bring the plants inside and place them in a bright, cool space. Avoid putting them near a radiator as they will dry out. They will start flowering within three weeks.

9. After flowering indoors, the hyacinths can be planted outdoors and they will bloom the following spring.

Shake a rainstick

Listen to the sound of rain

What you need:

- Sturdy cardboard tubes such as foil, cling film or poster tubes (kitchen towel rolls are too soft)
- Hammer and nails, cocktail sticks
- A poster tube lid or plastic milk bottle lid
- Glue and tape
- Beans, corn kernels, dry rice, seeds or little stones
- Decorating materials: paper, foil, stickers, glitter, beads, pens, paint

Top tip

Make music with the rainstick and other musical instruments and try some rain dancing.

What's in it for the children?

This is a good creative activity. Working together to design and make the rainstick and then using it to create musical rain.

Taking it forward

- Start a rain project. Place a rain gauge in the garden to measure the rainfall.
- Make some other natural musical instruments. Use empty gourds filled with dried beans into maracas. Cut bamboo into pairs of claves or tapping sticks.

What to do:

1. Traditionally rain sticks were instruments made from hollow cacti, thorns and tiny pebbles and were used to invoke the rain spirits.

2. Although we are not usually short of rain in this country, it's important that the children understand the importance of rain in keeping gardens alive.

3. Choose a sturdy cardboard tube. Poster tubes are best because they often come with a lid.

4. Carefully, push or hammer some nails or cocktail sticks into the tube. The more sticks you tap in, the longer it will take for the beans to fall through, making the noise of the rain last longer.

5. Use the lid to seal one end or glue a plastic milk bottle lid to the end if you are using a smaller tube. Fasten it securely to stop the rain escaping.

6. Fill with some rice or beans making sure the sticks don't trap them. Seal the open end of the tube.

7. Decorate the outside of the rain stick with collage materials, pens, stickers or paint with colourful images of bees, flowers and butterflies.

8. Listen to the sound of the rain stick.

Take flight

Making a paper airplane

What you need:

- A4 paper
- Patience
- Space to test planes!

Top tip ⭐

Encourage the children to try not to get cross if their airplanes won't fly! Let the children practise using scrap paper, persevere and try again.

What to do:

1. Try this traditional activity in the garden, folding and flying model airplanes. It's a cheaper and easier alternative to making and flying kites.

2. Start with a plain piece of A4 paper.

3. Fold the paper in half lengthwise, make a good strong crease and unfold.

4. With the paper in a portrait orientation in front of you, fold both of the top corners down to the middle crease to make a basic 'house' shape, i.e. a square with a triangle roof on top.

5. Fold the slanted edges down toward the middle crease.

6. Fold the right side over to the left side along the middle crease, making sure that all your folds are on the inside.

7. Fold the left edge back on itself to form a wing.

8. Turn the paper over and repeat.

9. Unfold the wings upwards slightly.

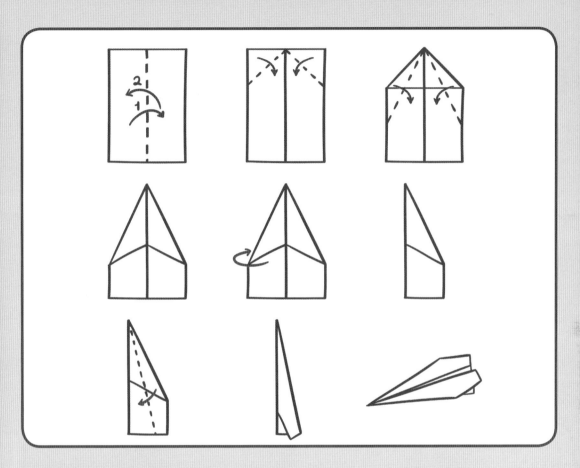

What's in it for the children?

This activity requires focus, determination and fine manipulation skills. These motor skills will aid the children when they are ready to write. They will also indirectly learn about forces and gravity.

Taking it forward

- Decorate the paper before making the airplane. Choose which is the best-decorated airplane.

- Use different kinds of paper such as origami paper, cardboard and newspaper.

- Hold a competition to see which airplane can fly the farthest.

- Try some other origami activities.

Stone numbers
Counting in the garden

What you need:

- 10 round flat stones as a starting point
- Permanent markers
- Varnish or PVA glue

Top tip ⭐

This activity also works with shells, colourful stones or crystals and challenges us to think differently about using ordinary natural items.

What's in it for the children?

Using natural materials to explore mathematical concepts and develop counting skills help the children gain more understanding.

Taking it forward

- Invite parents and families to collect the stones during walks, weekend trips or holidays and make a set of stone numbers to use at home. Just be clear about the best shapes and size to look for.

- Paint images of favourite story characters on the stones and use them as story props at circle time.

- Try a Helicopter session where the children sit in a circle and create a story beginning with 'Once upon a time'. The stone is their 'talking stone' and when they hold the stone they become the story tellers.

What to do:

1. Go on a walk with the children and families to collect stones from a stony beach, park or garden. Flat, round stones work best. Transform them into stone numbers.

2. Line the stones on the ground and write a number on each stone using a permanent marker. On the other side of the stones create the corresponding number of dots.

3. Seal the stones with varnish to preserve them.

4. Let children use the stones to count forwards and backwards, order numbers, recognise numbers, create number bonds, make up simple number sentences, and so on. The options are endless.

5. Learning about numbers requires lots of practice and children will enjoy practising in unusual places. Use the stone numbers inside, outside, in the sand tray, on the carpet, wherever the children take the lead.

Catch of the day
Fishing for fun

What you need:

- Fishing line
- Sturdy stick, up to 1 m long
- Safe scissors
- Metal S hooks
- A pond in the water tray – coloured water, paper weeds, shells, stones, moss, floating flowers
- Toy fish and other items to be fished out of the pond
- Dry pond, magnet, paperclips and cardboard fish

What's in it for the children?

Constructing the fishing rod and using it in a variety of situations will help the children develop hand-to-eye coordination. They will explore mathematical language with regards to size and shape. They can use tally charts to count their catch!

Taking it forward

- Write numbers, phonics or words on the reverse side of the cardboard fish so children can extend their learning by reading and counting the fish they catch.
- Introduce children to the idea of angling. Invite an interested parent or keen angler to visit and share their enthusiasm and information about fish with the children.
- Visit a local pet or exotic fish shop or take a trip to the Aquarium.
- Set up a fish tank in the nursery so children can find out about caring for tropical fish.

What to do:

1. Have some fun in the garden by going fishing.

2. Tie one end of the fishing line to the stick (use the thicker end of the stick as the handle). Wrap the line in a spiral around the stick until you reach the opposite tip. Tie the line firmly to the tip, but don't cut the line yet.

3. Unroll the line about 30 cm longer than the stick and cut it off the roll. You should have a continuous length of fishing line extending from the handle of the stick down to the hook.

4. Tie a hook to the end of the line. Now you're ready to fish!

5. If there is a pond in the garden, let the children have a go at fishing for weeds and other loose items. Who is the most successful fisherman?

6. Or, set up a pond in a water tray outside using coloured water and decorate it with paper weeds, shells, stones, moss and floating flowers. Put toy fish and other items that can be hooked in the water for the children to catch.

7. Alternatively, set up a dry pond in a tray using cardboard fish, boots, hats and other creatures. Fix a paper clip to each item. Attach a magnet to the fishing rod in place of the hook and try some magnetic fishing.

Top tip ⭐

The best type of stick to use for the fishing rod is strong, yet slightly flexible. Bamboo, about 1 cm thick, would be ideal.

Vegetable printing

Using up wonky vegetables

What you need:

- Suitable vegetables: potatoes, carrots, parsnips, okra, celery, sweetcorn, cauliflower, artichokes, mushrooms
- Ribbon
- Cookie cutters or shapers
- Knife
- Paint
- Paper or cardboard

Top tip

When you have run out of suitable vegetables let the children carry on printing with the cookie cutters.

What's in it for the children?

This activity provides lots of opportunity for creativity, recognising shapes and patterns and develops find motor control.

Taking it forward

- Try a group picture or try drawing a large tree trunk or vase and let the children print leaves and flowers onto the base using different vegetable shapes.

✚ Health & Safety

Don't let children handle sharp knives to cut the potatoes without supervision.

What to do:

1. Select some suitable vegetables. Try to use vegetables from the nursery garden or buy ones that have passed their sell by date or are classified as 'wonky'.

2. Use carrots or parsnips cut both ways, to print circles and rectangles.

3. Tie a bunch of celery with a ribbon and cut the ends. Use it like a paint brush. Dip into the paint and print a range of images and patterns.

4. Find out what shape okra makes when printed.

5. Use a corn on the cob rolled on its side to get a great pattern. Try a range of interesting vegetables such as artichokes, squash, broccoli, cauliflower, kohlrabi and celeriac.

6. Potatoes are great for printing and can be cut into different shapes. Cut a potato in half and press a cookie cutter into the cut edge. Use a sharp knife to cut away the potato right up to the cutter.

7. Dip the potato shapes into shallow trays of different coloured paint and make some prints. Watch how the prints fade as they are repeated.

Milk bottle top mobile

Decorating the garden

What you need:

- Plastic milk bottle tops in blue, green and red
- Scissors and string
- Fir cones
- Wooden or metal coat hanger

Top tip ⭐

Nurseries drink a lot of milk, so this is a good way to recycle materials such as bottle tops.

What's in it for the children?

Children will enjoy handling tools and using a variety of materials to make decorations for the garden.

Taking it forward

- Use foil or metal bottle tops to make more mobiles for the garden and listen to the sounds they make.
- String up different lengths of hollow bamboo and suspend them from nylon fishing line. They make a lovely clunky sound when blown by the wind.
- Make a mobile to use as a scarecrow to keep birds off the seeds. Suspend CDs on string so they catch the sun as they move and scare off birds.

✚ Health & Safety

Adults can pierce holes in the plastic tops using a metal nail or skewer and hammer or a hot needle.

What to do:

1. Encourage the children to think about decorating the garden with their own artwork or creations. This is good way to connect indoor and outdoor activities.

2. Make a collection of different-coloured milk bottle tops. Pierce holes in each top.

3. Ask the children to make a pattern with the coloured tops. Try splitting up the colours into three sets or create a repeating pattern.

4. Cut lengths of string and thread the tops onto them. Try different lengths of string.

5. Sequence the tops by colour or thread them together on one long string with a fir cone attached at the bottom.

6. Fix the strings to the hanger.

7. Choose a good place to hang them such as a tree, a strong bush with large branches, in the entrance porch or from the fence.

8. Make sure that you hang them where you can see them!

Singing in the garden

Singing and dancing outside

What you need:

- Songs and nursery rhymes to celebrate being in the garden
- Camera or tablet
- Card and pen
- Singing bucket

Top tip ⭐

Print out a song sheet so children can sing the songs at home with their families. Ask parents or grandparents to share any songs about gardens that they know.

What's in it for the children?

Singing together is an important part of making music and expressing ideas through songs, rhythm and rhyme.

Taking it forward

- Encourage children to make up their own words to familiar tunes.

- Photograph or film the children singing. Get permission from parents and put the film on the website.

What to do:

1. Try to give the children a sense that the garden is place where they can enjoy themselves.

2. Create space and time so children can run, jump, roll, tumble, spin, skip and enjoy the freedom of being outside in the garden.

3. Start a regular outside singing time. Use circle time to gather the children into a group.

4. Here are some favourites songs and rhymes to start with:

   - *In and Out the Dusty Bluebells*
   - *Mary, Mary, Quite Contrary*
   - *Here We Go Round the Mulberry Bush*
   - *This is My Garden, I'll Plant it with Care*
   - *Lavender's Blue (Dilly Dilly)*

5. Write the names of the songs and rhymes onto cards and place in a 'singing bucket' for children to pick from.

6. Try adding actions and dances to the songs.

The tyre garden

What you need:

- Tyres – all sizes (motor bikes to tractors)
- Aprons
- Emulsion paint
- Wide paint brushes
- Soil, multi-purpose compost
- Selection of plants – tomato plants, herbs

What to do:

1. Get some old tyres from your nearest garage or recycling centre. Try asking families and friends; it's surprising how many people keep old tyres. They are a good alternative if garden space is limited.

2. Help children to decorate the tyres with different-coloured paints. Leave to dry between coats.

3. Fill the middle of the tyre with soil and add a layer of top soil to provide nutrients. Add some multi-purpose compost.

4. Plant your chosen flowers or herbs. Place the tyre in the right place for your chosen plants, for instance choose a sunny space if you plant tomatoes.

5. Water and feed the plants regularly.

Top tip ⭐

If you have lots of tyres, decorate each one differently and stack or hang them around. Make a small tyre into a hanging basket.

What's in it for the children?

They will enjoy conversations about recycling tyres and rubber and can compare the decoration, size and patterns of the tyres.

Taking it forward

- Use tyres in lots of different ways. Make a tyre swing and hang it from a suitable tree. Stuff a round cushion into the centre to make outside seats and create a reading space. Place some tyres in a row for children to climb and clamber on.

- Make a collection of small tyres or vehicles and use them to print tyre patterns. Press into a shallow tray of paint and drive across the paper.

The garden treasure hunt

Round and round the garden

What you need:

- Treasure to hide in the garden: plastic animals, tins of coins, chocolate money or wine gums
- Spade or trowel
- A set of clues to help find the treasure

Top tip ⭐

Start the activity with an indoor treasure hunt. Ask children to sit in a circle, hide a toy in the room and guide the seeker to find it using 'hot and cold'.

What's in it for the children?

This activity encourages children to use observation skills and follow verbal and picture clues.

Taking it forward

- Organise the children into teams. Use a timer and challenge them to finish the hunt in a set time. Which team can find the most items? Make badges for the winners and certificates.

➕ Health & Safety

Remind children not to touch anything dirty or sharp or to talk to strangers. Tell them to look out for plants while hunting so they don't trample everything underfoot.

What to do:

1. A treasure hunt in the garden requires planning and a set of clues and hints to help the players find the treasure.

2. Go into the garden and bury the treasure: plastic dinosaurs, animals, cars, tins of coins or jewellery, sealed containers of chocolate money, wine gums or other sweets.

3. Remember not to make the hunt too tricky. For small children who can't read, the clues need to be sensible such as 'getting hot' or 'going cold' or picture clues. Place staff strategically around the garden to help children who are struggling.

4. Give the children a list of things to look for. The possibilities are endless. Link it to topics or interests of the children. Here are a few ideas:

   - Metal objects, coins, jewellery
   - Wildlife, worms, snails, slugs,
   - Plastic dinosaurs
   - Cinderella's slipper
   - Space rocks (white stones).

A nursery garden scrapbook

Creating a storybook of outside adventures

What you need:

- Scrapbooks
- Paper
- Felt pens and crayons
- Glue
- Leaves and plants
- Sticky-backed plastic
- Paints
- Camera
- Seed catalogues
- Scissors

Top tip ⭐

Create a display for the nursery wall using the scrapbook as the basis of the design. Publish some of the photos and features on your website.

What's in it for the children?

This activity involves children in creating a storybook of their journey to becoming gardeners with evidence of all their learning on the way – designing and planning, growing and caring for plants and working together.

Taking it forward

- Ask other people in the nursery, family and visitors to write their impressions of the garden to add to the book.

- Display the scrapbook in the book corner for children to look at and to impress any 'important visitors'.

What to do:

1. Celebrate progress made by making a scrapbook to tell the story of how to create a garden. It can be a group scrapbook or children can make individual scrapbooks.

2. Ask children to draw pictures of themselves in the garden, write their name and date and stick it on the first page of their scrapbook.

3. Collect leaves and plants from the garden and put them in the scrapbook. Don't choose thick, fleshy samples, as they will rot. Some samples can be pressed and dried quickly using a microwave oven.

4. Help children to cover samples with sticky-backed plastic.

5. Draw or paint pictures of different parts of the garden and take photographs.

6. Choose one part of the garden and take a picture of it on the first day of each month for a year. Children can see how much everything changes.

7. Encourage children to keep their scrapbook near a window so they can draw or write the names of the birds or other wildlife coming into the garden over the different seasons.

8. Stick in the seed packets of any seeds grown in the scrapbook. Cut out pictures from seed catalogues of plants they have grown.

9. Include plans for the future. Which plants would they like to grow next? Design a dream garden!

Useful organisations

What you need:

Information about:

- The Woodland Trust – www.woodlandtrust.org.uk

- RSPB (Royal Society for the Protection of Birds) – www.rspb.org.uk

- The Canal & River Trust – www.canalrivertrust.org.uk

- The Wildlife Trusts – www.wildlifetrusts.org

- Buglife – www.buglife.org.uk

- www.earthrestorationservice.org (This conservation organisation donates free flowers, plants and trees to schools)

- www.schoolgardening.rhs.org.uk (The Royal Horticultural Society runs this useful website to help school gardeners)

- www.countrysideclassroom.org.uk

What to do:

1. If gardening or caring for plants and wildlife is new to you, join an organisation that has been set up to help.

2. Organisations such as the Woodland Trust and RSPB are there to encourage, support and educate people about trees, birds and wildlife. They are a brilliant way to access up to date information and ideas for staff, children and their families. The organisations mentioned are just a handful of the many local and national charities that can provide ideas, information, events and experiences.

3. Choose an organisation that is relevant to where you are. If you're near a river you might join The Canal & River trust. If you're near a forest, try the Woodland Trust.

4. Check the organisation does activities that work for young children such as BBC's Springwatch or the annual RSPB Big Garden Birdwatch.

5. Go with what the children are particularly interested in, so if they are fascinated by minibeasts join Buglife.

Top tip

Joining an organisation is only worthwhile if you use what it has to offer, so try to include activities in the yearly calendar.

What's in it for the children?

Being involved with one of these organisations will provide a broad educational experience and many exciting activities that the children will benefit from throughout their lives.

Taking it forward

- If you cannot afford to join these groups, organise a fundraising activity to earn the membership fee.

- Select them as a chosen charity and raise funds by selling Christmas cards, holding a plant or cake sale or selling calendars with photographs of the children in the garden.